REQUIEM

Javier A. Robayo

New England Endeavors

N.E.E.
Clinton, CT 06413

Cover Art Work by Digital Art Designs (DAD)
Ansonia, Connecticut
Copyright © 2013 Jaime Robayo
All Rights Reserved.
ISBN-10:0989107620
ISBN-13:978-0-9891076-2-4

Dedication

For my Shelton High School classmates, Christopher Papp and Joseph Budahazy. Thank you for touching my life.

REQUIEM

-1-

Rain dampens the mound of fresh earth that covers the newest grave in the grounds of Seaside Memorial Cemetery in Stratford. Only when the chill forces its way through my head and into my spine, do I realize I'm the last person still standing next to Steve's grave.

Aside from the grief and the unwarranted sense of injustice, I've run through a list of questions in a futile attempt to explain the inexplicable.

I've stared for a long time at the inscription on the elegant slab of marble that will mark the grave, uncomfortable with the finality it represents but at least, it's over.

My best friend, Steve Rand, died a slow, agonizing death as his family stood by, guilt-ridden and conflicted. I don't think they knew whether to ask God for the cancer to leave his body or for it to just kill him once and for all.

They had no business making it about themselves. At first, I resented them for doing just that but then again, I was not the one helplessly watching the slow decay of his body and spirit for over a year. I failed to see him even once through that difficult time. I get to remember Steve as I saw him last: robust, healthy, and full of life.

I can say I was busy with my own laundry list of calamities but even if I'd lived next door to Steve, I would not have seen him often.

My best friend worked himself to death so his second wife could ride a silver Mercedes into the garage of their mansion in Westport, and so his stepson could throw away his education at Fairfield Prep. The kid now spends his time at home, still partying the way he has since he came into Steve's wealth when he was seventeen, though with less friends. Most of them were in attendance because they liked and respected Steve, not necessarily to offer their comfort to young Carson, whose notable absence spoke volumes of the poor relationship he cultivated with his stepdad. To be fair, it's not all on the kid's shoulders. His mother had him at fifteen and he grew up with more of an older sister than a mother. I often joked Steve left Marney to raise two kids.

I suppose I've no right to cast stones. I wonder if my own son would so easily opt out of seeing me one last time, even if only to say good bye as my body was lowered to the ground.

"'Scuse me, Sir. Ain't you gots no home to go to?"

"Pardon me?" I turn to find a thin, stooped man propping a dirty hat on kinked hair grizzled with age. He pronounces the word Sir "Suh." The drawl is thick and the cadence brings to mind the muddy beauty of the Mississippi.

"Morty don't mean no disrespect, but these folks all gots to rest forever, and you being here ain't helpin' 'em none ."

I allow a tight smile to hide my annoyance. "Rest?" I scoff. "That's one way of putting it."

The man shuffles away a few steps then stops and surveys the sky. A reddish stain on the left shoulder of his shirt draws my attention.

"You gonna catch yourself your death in the downpour comin'. Gots to get you home."

He doesn't see me roll my eyes in reply as I look at my watch; 3:31P.M.

Rays of sunlight still stab the grounds through random spots where the clouds don't fuse. This man just wants me out of here so he can get back to whatever it is gravediggers do after a burial.

"Sir, Mister Rand says you gots to stop being a stubborn fool and get yourself home. Listen to Morty." He points at himself. "Morty ain't never wrong 'bout these things."

For a second, I think I misunderstood his first statement. The hair at the back of my neck stands on end and a chill courses through my body. The sensation quickly passes however as logic overrides it. "Morty, is that your name?"

"Sure is, Sir. Sure is."

Morty's dark skin is as taut as a drum over his skull though carefully lined with age. Each crease is a line in a book about a long, hard life. Watery, jaundiced eyes take turns scrutinizing me. He reminds me of a pug I once knew whose eyes drifted away from each other so badly the mutt actually turned its head so it could walk a straight line.

If I were still writing, Morty would make a great character in a novel as the gravedigger who fancies himself a necromancer. "What else does Mr. Rand say?" I decide to humor him.

The man blinks unevenly and glances at the darkening sky as though looking for a sign from heaven. He becomes so enthralled with the clouds I end up glancing upward as well.

"Mr. Rand says you gots to listen to them ol' voices in your head and get on writing."

The last conversation I had with Steve was marked by his insistence for me to listen to the voices in my head. It was how he referred to my writing after I explained how characters tend to write a story rather than the author. How would this cemetery man know about that? Lucky guess?

I heard from a woman at the diner I visited before the funeral that the local church supports programs for the mentally challenged. According to the woman, the pastor often hired the few souls that have their shit mostly together. Morty might have just made the cut and I sense his "ability" to hear the dead made him a shoe-in for the job.

"Better get inside, Mister Ken."

I frown. I don't remember giving Morty my name, but that same little shred of logic that calmed me somewhat just moments ago, allows me to assume he heard someone call out to me although I don't remember much talking taking place. Friends and relatives merely shared awkward silences and the universal sad nod required for the occasion. If it weren't for his non-rhotic southern drawl, I'd probably let my imagination get the best of me and see a threat where there is none.

Morty's eyes turn eerily white when lightning flashes behind me, slicing open the clouds' pregnant bellies.

A second later, the apocalyptic crack that shakes the earth makes me jump out of my skin and heavy rain drenches me within a breath.

I've dropped the umbrella I carried with me. It's okay. Opening it now would be like waving a red cape at the bull in the sky.

The rain is so thick it hampers my vision. I'd run for my car except that I'd end up running in circles, and that's only if I didn't collide against a tombstone or a tree.

"This way!" Morty grips my arm and leads me in a mad dash toward a block building I don't remember seeing until we are within ten feet of it.

The old man is amazingly quick, far more than I would expect at first sight. With a swift kick from his boot, Morty opens the door. A few seconds later a bare light bulb flickers above me before throwing us into darkness once more.

Morty strikes a match and works quickly to light up tall thick candles like the ones flanking church altars. His shadow dances on the wall to the rhythm of the lambent light.

"You shoulda listened to ol' Morty," he grumbles, shaking his head. "I gets you a towel."

I watch him scurry away through an old shower curtain used in lieu of a door that leads to the back of the small building.

The sky roars after another jagged bolt rips it apart. I wonder what happens to the unfortunate raindrops caught in the lightning bolt's way. Do they vaporize? Maybe they come to the end of their brief existence before they can complete their journey to the soil where we are all meant to end up.

"Here, Mister Ken. Yous ought to peel off that long coat before you gets the flu or some other bug. I gots me tea in the kettle, warm ourselves up some."

The man's Southern drawl and hospitality put a smile on my face. It's been a long time since I've been able to engage in an easy chat with a friend. I realize I'm taking advantage of the fact this man doesn't know me from Adam. If he did, he would have left me in the rain. "Thank you, Morty."

The man grins like a child and nods in appreciation of my gratitude. "Mr. Rand says he proud of you. Yous a good man, he says."

This new strange statement presents me with a few choices: Risk drowning in the deluge, possibly get incinerated by lighting or continue to chat with my new friend, the necromancer. "I try, Morty."

His smile fades as he fixes me with one eye while the other one focuses on the door. "He says you ought to try harder though."

I shrug out of my damp coat and find a wooden stool where I park my bones. "I imagine he's right."

Morty pulls a plastic milk crate. He turns it upside down and appears to settle in for a long talk I suddenly dread, and that's when it hits me…

Not a single drop of rain darkens the fabric of his clothes.

-2-

"I likes me this here black tea. Black tea for a black man. Ain't that right?" He chuckles.

Rain hisses on the softer ground and batters the tar roof and the window panes in a staccato that grows more comforting by the minute despite its violence.

Morty crosses his thin legs and somehow manages not to flatten the sharp crease of his khakis. His fingers wrap around a chipped mug he rests on his lap. Neither eye is aimed my way.

"How old are you, Morty?"

"Ah," he sighs. "Ol' Morty be older than time, he be. Ain't no spring chicken like Mister

Ken." He stares at me for a moment. "Three tens and a seven, ain't it?"

Morty wavers in my vision until I blink. "That's right. I'm thirty-seven."

He slaps at the air. "Hell son, you ain't lived nothin'. Shit…" He sips his tea.

I barely contain my surprise at the sudden condescension in his tone. Less than a whole sentence ago, I was Mister Ken. How did I become *son*?

"Lots of folks dead out there."

I follow the eye that's not staring at the wall to my left. Outside, the stone markers are impervious to the torrent, like guards at the tomb of the Unknown Soldier.

Cemeteries depress me, not for the obvious reasons but their utter uselessness. At some point, a grave stops having visitors, and no one comes by to leave a bouquet of dead flowers or even to remove the weeds. Spouses move on and often find someone else. Children promise to visit all the time but before they know it, life rolls on and obligations get in the way of their good intentions. And grandchildren? Forget it. Eventually, the visits stop and only a person like Morty is left to tend to the grave once in a while.

What a frightening loneliness.

"You scared of dying?"

I take a sip of the hot tea, scalding my mouth as I debate on a long, verbose reply but sensing how important my answer may be, I offer the truth. "Every day, Morty. You?"

He waves his hand. "I ain't afraid of nothing, least of all old Grim Reaper hisself."

"You're braver than me."

"Brave?" Morty frowns like a father whose patience is gone. "Brave ain't gots nothing to do with nothing. Brave's just another word for stupid."

I chuckle uneasily, wondering whether I've offended him. "I wouldn't call you stupid, Morty."

The sudden anger ebbs from him. "What yous come here for?"

"Me?"

He nods. "All yous."

I shrug. "To pay our respects. To say goodbye. You know that."

Morty stares at me as he nods slowly. "That's what folks says. I hear all kinds of nice things about them folks in them caskets, but why yous wait so long to say them nice things?"

Nothing is simple about his question. My answer is far too complicated so I offer him a generality. "It's the human way, I guess."

"If we all gots to die to hear some nice things said bout us then that's just sad."

"I think you're right, but you wouldn't hear a thing. You're dead."

Morty grins. "You be somewheres," he argues. "Shit. I knows."

I like the sound of his laughter. It rings with the honesty few friendships enjoy. Nothing like the suppressed, phony half-chuckles that pointed the quick conversations I had a few hours ago with people I've known most of my adult life.

"Look at yourself. Yous one lonely cuz." He shakes his head. "Gots a wife?

For a second, I take offense but my *none of your damn business* melts into a pathetic mumbling. "I used to."

"She dead?"

I shake my head. "She's dead in here," I reply, tapping the left pocket of my shirt."

"I thinks it's that other ways round. I be sure it's your fault, I reckon."

If anyone else said that, I would vehemently defend my position and cast the blame on Kate. She gave up on me, after all.

"Look at you getting all mad like a wet cat. Grudges don't do nobody no good."

A small puddle has formed under the cuffs of my slacks which continue to drip. Morty has no such problem. He must have changed when he went into the backroom I think, dismissing the eeriness I felt upon realizing his clothes were not wet. Everything has an explanation.

If he was taller and broader, I'd ask him to lend me some dry pants.

One of his watery eyes dances on each of mine. "Miz Kate ain't give up on nothing. You's a damn fool."

I couldn't be more shocked if Morty grew another head right before my very eyes. "How do you even know my wife's name?"

"Morty knows."

His enigmatic gaze pisses me off. "Who have you been talking to? How do you know Kate?"

His smile is downright feral, his gaze far from amused.

"Did you just raise your voice at me, son? Never you mind how Morty knows. Morty just knows."

Driven by indignation, I intend to stand and scream at the man. My ire evaporates when a flicker of fire dances along his eyes.

I freeze.

What the hell kind of optical illusion was that?

Morty blinks. I look for that sudden strangeness but the eyes staring at me are as black as pools of ink.

"Was time she quit talking to the wall you gone done become is all."

I drop my gaze under the weight of the truth in his words, more than a little stunned. "Why do you say that?" I ask haltingly.

"Ain't no good woman gonna bash her head against a wall very long. Sooner or later she gonna quit. Good peoples ain't no martyrs."

Thunder rumbles as though to punctuate the man's irritating statements.

"You know what a martyr is?"

"I be looking at one this very damn second." He chuckles without much humor.

"What are you talking about?"

Bemused, Morty stands slowly. The effort makes him sigh deeply. "Mister Ken, yous finally seeing yourself in a mirror."

"How do you know my wife's name?"

Morty dismisses my question with an exaggerated shrug. "You ain't gots to be no martyr."

I don't even pretend to understand I'm so angry. "I'm no martyr."

"Yous convinced yourself of that, I reckon. Gonna take more than ol' Morty to set your ass straight."

We look out the window for a long moment as the heavens continue in their mad efforts to cleanse the world. Morty walks up to the window and pushes away at the worn curtain on the rod. The gnarled hand has fingers that end in curved talons. As he turns, his hand drops and disappears from view only to reappear under his chin. His fingernails look surprisingly clean and trimmed once again.

There's no way I just imagined that.

If anyone would've told me I'd spend the night of Steve's funeral with a ghost or whatever Morty is, I would've laughed in their face. "Why did you bring me here?"

"Yous tell me. Yous be the one afraid."

Any normal person would grab his coat and run out of the dank place, but an eerie sense of calm convinces me to stay and talk. I actually feel safe in the company of this man…

Or whatever he is.

"Yes…" Morty nods slowly. "Now you be coming around."

Lightning produces a disjointed series of stark flashes that appear to reveal a bare skull where Morty's face should be.

"What's going on? What is this?" Fear coils in the pit of my stomach.

Morty smiles. "What you think of dying?"

"What's that got to do with anything?" I ask in exasperation.

Menace colors his grin as a silvery flash dances over his eyes. It's so fleeting I think I imagined it.

"What you think of dying?"

I'm done. I want out of here.

"Not before you talk," he says sternly when I glance at the door.

I'm at a loss. "Dying? Dying is not fair."

He stares with interest. "Don't think so? Why?"

"It just causes a lot of pain."

"Pain *is* life. Dying? Hell that be nothing but some well-deserved rest."

"Dying is becoming nothing. I don't want to die." The truth in my voice startles me.

"Well," Morty says, clasping his arthritic hands. "Now that be the first time you lied today."

My breath grows shallow when he focuses on me. His sudden intensity unnerves me. "What about you, Morty?" I ask in a tremulous voice. "What was it like?"

Morty cocks his head. "Which time?"

-3-

My name is Ken, Kenneth Glass. I'm an author or at least, I wanted to be. I have a business or at least, I used to. I live in a warm and cozy home or at least, I had one. I have a lovely wife or at least I once did. I'm my little boy's hero or at least, he used to think of me as his hero. I have an enviable life or at least, I used to…

I ought to omit that entire last paragraph, but I'm sure a reason exists to justify the badly composed bio born out of a desire to look in the mirror and separate fact from fiction, sorrow from joy.

The meager possessions that managed to find their way into the small chamber where I sleep, speak of another lifetime I don't care to recall.

I left the rocky beaches of Connecticut for the woodlands of Oregon after my wife decided to quit "bashing her head against the wall," as Morty put it.

I'm back in Stratford because my lifelong friend succumbed to cancer. When I received that telephone call from his ex-wife, I offered no reaction. I sensed Marney didn't approve of my callousness but she was wrong in her assumption. It sucked that Steve died but as the cliché goes, he left for a better place and his suffering is finally over.

"Ain't no trip to yesterday gonna clear your mind. Dump the junk out your head."

Morty scuttles in his small kitchen, banging pots and knocking over glassware. I should leave but I'm compelled to stay. I really have no place to go.

"It don't do no good to dig up the past. Ain't no point in carrying it around. It will only weigh you down so you damn well better keep swimming, boy. It don't matter how deep the waters of trouble are if yous keep on swimming."

Needing some time to absorb his words, I take a cooler sip of tea, and glance around the rickety pieces of mismatched furniture. A small glass box sits on the marred top of an end table. The heart and the purple ribbon within surprise me. "You're a soldier?"

Morty looks annoyed at the change of subject. "Somebody was." A sad shake of his head. "187th infantry regiment, I reckon."

"It sounds familiar." I rack my brains for a reference, but I draw a blank.

"Them's the boys died up there on Hamburger Hill in sixty-nine. Them's gone made a movie about it. Got most of it wrong, but folks seemed to like it enough."

"Is it yours?"

Morty shrugs. "Could be."

In the corner of the room, leaning against a moldy armoire, a wooden spear catches my eye. Before I get the chance to ask, he clears his throat and continues to talk.

"Them boys…" he speaks in a hollow voice. "Ain't none of them fought for God or country or the fat cats in D.C. when they was there.

Those boys just wanted to live. Ain't that something?"

"How do you know that?"

He shrugs.

I have not come across too many veterans willing to discuss their time "in country." I don't question it. It's nothing I could ever relate to. The closest I've been to a similar situation is the last time I went hunting with my father in Western Pennsylvania.

While we waited for some dumb deer to venture within shooting range, we had one of those long chats. Meaning of life kind of stuff. I was gibbering about my plans after college when he grew less attentive, his eyes scanning the trees.

I tried to get his attention when he went suddenly still and clutched his rifle tighter while I froze when a cougar growled low in his throat before charging me.

I didn't even get a scratch, but the pulsing waves of terror didn't die when Dad shot the big cat. To this day, I'm not sure what I was most afraid of: the cougar or the shot? I knew then, I'd never cut it as a soldier.

"They was ghosts, them little yellow men. They was good at killing. You be minding your own business and out of the muthafucking ground one gone jump up and take down GI's. Left them boys screaming for their mommas." He swipes at the air in front of him. "Ain't none of our boys killed the yellow men in the name of God, liberty, and country. Them boys just wanted to gets home."

"This is what they told you?"

"It don't matter. Ain't nobody talks about that war. That *losing* war. Shit..." Morty scoffs. "Ain't nobody wins no goddamn war."

"The Vietnamese won that one."

Morty whips his head around to look at me. Both of his eyes look straight at me. "You thick or something? You ax one of them Mamasans lost her boy, her daddy, her husband. You ax her what she won."

He's right. No one wins a war. The winners only justify the bloodshed. "I can't even imagine."

"Oh, but you can. You done good on that paperback you wrote."

A cold current swirls through my gut. Lightning flashes and once again, the strobe effect distorts Morty's features into a macabre, demonic mask.

"What are you, an angel or a demon? How do you know what I wrote?"

He grins. "Morty knows things." He taps his temple.

When I was twenty, I self-published a short story about a young soldier who returned from Vietnam and saw ghosts from the war everywhere he looked. It wasn't a horrible piece, but it went nowhere. No big deal. I was only trying to impress my friends with a book with my name on it. The vanity publisher was more than happy to take my money and hand me a box of books. "How'd you get your hands on my short story?"

"Did me some time in the big house ages ago. Ain't nothing to do but read. Ain't none too proud of that, but life's life."

"Sounds like you've lived quite a life, Morty."

"Lawd knows that's right." He pauses. "A few of them."

Anyone else would deem this man crazy, but perhaps I'm the one going crazy. "What were you in for?"

He shakes his head. "It don't matter now." He steeples his fingers and leans his elbows on his thighs. He doesn't move much but he's suddenly closer. "We be here cuz of you."

I wonder if that *We* includes me.

-4-

"I seen death lots o' times. It's a pretty sight."

"How can death possibly be a pretty sight?"

He ignores my outraged tone. "What you think a sunset is?"

My head spins. "Sunset?"

He nods. "That there's the death of daytime and that's a pretty sight we see just about each day."

"That's not a death. It's just day becoming night."

"Yeah?"

"Yes."

"Do you gets that day back? Once a Monday becomes a Tuesday, you ain't never get *that* Monday again. That Monday be dead," he states with the finality of Salomon passing judgment.

"No. It just passed and it comes back in another week."

A sad shake of his head. "Ain't no one Monday be like another Monday."

I'm still running lines in my head about the death of days when I barely hear Morty ask me something. "I'm sorry, what was that?"

Morty grins. "I axed, you like them tunes?"

"Music?"

He nods. "I likes me some of that fast Zydeco. Ain't nothing like it."

Add ADHD to Morty's list of traits. "Are we talking about music now?"

"Shit, no. We talking death here."

I try to gauge his mental stability, but I'm the one twitching under his scrutiny. Why am I still here? "I thought you just said—"

"Sure you like them tunes. You sing out your heart when you be driving your poppa's old truck."

I'm stunned but I smile, in part because I'm beginning to get used to Morty reading my mind or whatever this is and in part, because every now and then I hear a song that will make me feel so alive. Most of those times, I was driving my father's '63 GMC pickup. "Maybe I do."

Morty smiles, his teeth appear to glow in the dark canvas of his face. "Songs die too. Them all gots an end."

"Yeah, but you can play a song again."

He exhales like he's tired. "You be missing the point."

"What point?"

"Ain't even the prettiest things last forever except God hisself." Morty suddenly stands then bends at the waist and looms over me. "You know I'm saying?"

"I get it. No one lives forever," I reply quickly like a wayward schoolboy.

Morty sighs deeply, releasing the intensity from just seconds before. He sits once again and his eyes focus on some spot past either of my shoulders.

"Difference between you and everybody else is you so worried about dying, you gone done stopped living."

I don't refute his point. "I messed up my life, Morty, but that doesn't mean I stopped living."

He looks pleased. "Go on."

"What do you mean?"

"This be as frank as you ever been. Now keep talking. It be good for your soul."

"You want to know how I messed up my life?"

Morty nods.

"I thought you could read minds."

"You ain't hearing your own damn inner voice. Maybe if you hear your mouth talking, you might actually learn something. Go on now."

How convenient. "You already know everything about me, don't you?" Rebellion makes me stand and start for the door.

"Sit your ass back down, son!"

I turn to give the impertinent little man a final piece of my mind but he's disappeared.

The grip around the back of my neck is far stronger than what I expect out of an old gravedigger.

"Sit and talk to Morty. Quit being a damn fool."

"Ow!" I cry as he finally releases me.

"Ow? What's a matter, baby? Little pinch left a booboo?" He says in a little boy's voice that chills my blood. The voice is oddly familiar.

Rubbing my neck, I glare at the man after he deposits me back on the stool.

Morty threatens to backhand me. The move is so sudden I flinch.

"Don't you eyeball me like that again, boy, I'll slap you into next Sunday."

I drop my gaze like a scolded servant.

"Where you gonna go?"

"Home," I reply.

"You ain't got no home."

"You asked."

"You lied."

I did. I had a liquor store in mind.

"Nah ah." Morty shakes a spindly forefinger at me. "You ain't got the stomach for that. Ain't no answers at the bottoms of them whisky bottles. I knows. I looked and only found a wino muthafuckah staring back from the mirror. Is that what you want?"

Ghost or not, I'm done getting pushed around. "You were a drunk? I'm not surprised. Maybe that's why you make no sense. Do you need a drink? You could drink with me, you old con. What do you say? Let's get trashed. Let's get stupid."

The air around me grows suddenly artic and my flesh pebbles in response. An unseen vice squeezes my torso. When I look at Morty, his eyes are no longer staring in different directions. They're fixed on me and probably seeing right into my soul. His grin is a wide, demonic display of long, wickedly sharp teeth.

I credit the strobe effect of the lighting outside for the reptilian amber glow of his eyes. After a moment, his eyes turn black as empty space.

"You are upsetting me, boy."

Gone is the Southern drawl. Each word is perfectly enunciated and full of menace.

My mouth goes dry at the strange sight before me. The eeriness in the dead expression curdles my blood and I have trouble finding my voice. "I…apologize, Morty."

The sinister grin on his face remains as he accepts with a terse nod. If he rolled out a forked tongue, it would only complete the image and it wouldn't surprise me much. "You want me to talk? Okay, I'll talk."

"I be waiting."

-5-

I tell Morty that my life is no different than most people I know. I graduated high school a jackass and majored in what would make me money like a jackass. Every yuppie friend of mine did the same thing and now they bitch about stocks during their tennis games on Sundays.

Steve Rand was one of those guys.

He planned every aspect of his life. He even went after the most promising mate in Marney, heiress to the business empire of our Financial Theory professor, the venerable Dr. Donald Garrison.

Marney dragged her roommate Kate Hartwell to a double date which Steve agreed on my behalf. The date proved to be no hardship and it became a frequent event.

Kate was also a blue blood though she longed to get out from under her father's control which became easier when I, a kid from the wrong side of the tracks, asked for her hand.

Steve swept Marney off her feet at the onset, but two type A personalities seldom give up taking the lead in every aspect of their lives whether it's the house budget or who's on top of whom in bed.

Kate and I were a different story.

"She wasn't into the grand life. She could care less about the New York socialites. Kate wanted a quiet life; she wanted family game night…" A lump in my throat prevents me from going on.

"Yes. Yes, *now* you be talking."

The pang of longing gives way to a soft laugh I don't recognize as my own. "We got married."

"How'd you talk her into it?"

"I asked her to dance," I grin at the memory.

Morty slaps his thighs and cackles with delight. "Lawd! How'd Miz Kate gone done falling for the sorry likes of you?"

I shrug. "She found something I wrote."

"Ah," Morty stabs at the air above him. "Paul of the Night."

I'm speechless for a long moment. "Angel or demon, what are you, Morty?"

He only grins in response.

No one, not even Kate, knows that's the original title of the piece she read. "I gave it a different title."

Morty nods. "Corners." He shakes his head. "That's a goddamn shame, you ax me. All cuz some jackshit ain't liked your title. You has to know when to listen to yourself. Ain't you heard of instincts, and shit?"

"That jackshit, as you call him, is a published author who knows his business."

Morty harrumphs. "Published author, bah! He ain't nothing but a crowd pleaser, a muthafucking sell out."

"He's a New York Times bestseller. He wrote—"

"Shit. Cookie cutter shit. Give it time. Peoples ain't no fools. You'll see."

The finality in his voice invites no argument.

"Don't be acting like no goddamn star struck fool. One of your biggest problems is putting yourself below others. Only difference between you and that there fool is he gots his shit done while yous too afraid to get your shit done."

"It's not that," I protest.

"Get back to Miz Kate," he orders.

"What's the point?"

Morty drops his chin to his chest and fixes his right eye on me. An angry amber glow flashes in it. "Your ship ain't got no oars in the calm waters of your own regret."

I swallow hard before speaking. "What do you want from me?"

"I wants you to admit Miz Kate was the wind in your sails. Let's start there."

-6-

About the same time Marney and Steve started calling us to dish out their growing discontent with one another, Kate and I had never been more in love.

She spoke to her best friend from our bedroom while I listened to Steve moan about their lack of intimacy from the tiny living room in our Soho apartment . It was difficult to relate to him as Kate deliberately danced out of her clothes with a promising smile on her face, indicating I should wrap it up.

Making love to Kate took me to a different plane of existence. Bliss was always easily surpassed. She took me as often as I chased her.

We couldn't go very long without dropping our projects—along with our clothes—just to lose ourselves in each other's caresses.

A few years later, we were blessed with the news that we were having a son. By then, Steve and Marney had filed for divorce. They remained on friendly terms and we asked them to be our boy's godparents. They accepted.

Kate and I embarked on the adventure of parenthood. Those were the best days of my life…

"You hear the melody, can't you?"

Lost in my memories, I've almost forgotten Morty patiently listening to me gush about Kate's lovemaking. "Not sure what you mean, Morty."

He sighs and stares out the window.

Rain batters the panes and breaks up the lone light at the edge of the cemetery into a kaleidoscope that mimics my mind at this moment, full of memories of Kate.

"Ain't never can rain all the time."

"Yeah well, it can't be sunny all the time either."

"Lawd knows that's right. But if it was sunny all the days, you ain't never gonna learn to see them like a blessing." His eyes remain on the rain.

The near silence is soothing in spite of the eerie moments, too serene for two strangers discussing my life as though it's no more than the plot to a book.

"You be thinking like a writer. You should do what you be meant to do."

"I have bills to pay."

Morty turns to me. "Ain't we all?" He smiles but this time his teeth look small, ground to tiny nubs with two gaps where a couple used to be.

Light and shadows can play powerful mind tricks sometimes. Right?

Morty rubs his thighs before sinking into the back of an old, patched up couch. He looks frail and older somehow. "Can I get you a blanket?"

"You a kind man. Your momma raised a good boy."

Uncomfortable with the sudden praise, I reach for a raggedy, paper-thin afghan folded on a makeshift table and hand it to him.

"An old priest gave me this here blanket."

"Priests are kind."

"Priests are fools!" The vehemence in his voice takes me aback. "That brainwashed scum bribed me with this rag. You wanna know why?" He doesn't wait for an answer. "So I could find another place to sleep other than the cold stoop of his house of God hisself. He ain't wanted Morty to scare away the white peoples with money, see? That there fool ain't wanted to think of not having money for his mistress, see?"

"Not very Christian of him."

"Religion ain't nothing but a pretty veil for the selfish."

"There is no God," I reply, feeling a sudden sense of camaraderie with Morty that given the sour look on his face, is short lived.

"Boy, if you believe that nonsense then you a bigger fool than I thought."

"But you just said—"

"I says the truth!"

I have to laugh. "You confuse me, Morty."

"You only be confused cuz you got too much shit in them brains and can't think."

"Do you believe in God or not?"

Morty crosses his arms and glowers at me for a long moment before closing his eyes. After a while, I think he's asleep. I can finally leave.

"Sit your ass down, boy."

I almost roll my eyes but I don't want him threatening me again.

"Ax me again."

"Do you believe in God?"

"What yous said the first time baby boy smiled?"

"Huh?"

He curses me for a fool just under his breath. "That first time you held baby boy. What you said?"

"You tell me."

He looks impatient. "You get one free pass," he warns in that deep voice that scared me before as he studies me for a moment to make sure the threat is understood. "You said 'thank God, you were so worth the wait' that's what you said."

I actually hear my own voice uttering the sentiment. "What is this? Who are you?"

His demeanor is once again friendly. "You seen baby boy grow strong. The sun sets in those eyes of his, you tell me. God there?"

I nod in what I hope is a reverent way.

"That's right. Peoples got to stop listening to them money-hungry preaching muthafuckas in their fancy rags, standing at their fancy altars. Peoples got to quit giving them Sunday fools the time of day! Ain't nobody need no pastor telling them how to believe and what to believe. Yous got to believe it in here." He jabs at his heart. "Cuz once yous believe it in here, now you can live the way Jesus hisself says to live."

"Love thy neighbor…"

Morty nods once, slowly. "Yous a good boy, Mister Ken. Always was."

I've never seen this man until today, but he's accessed a vault in my soul I didn't even know I had.

Tears sting my eyes. "Why me, Morty? Why are we here talking like this? Why all the riddles?"

"Riddles?" Morty cocks his head and grins. "Real truth always sounds like riddles to you. Don't it?"

-7-

"I be here cuz this where I needs to be. You's here cuz Mister Rand got dead." Morty shrugs.

His callousness pisses me off. "Guess grave-digging makes death an everyday occurrence to some people."

"Lawd knows that's right. But I ain't some peoples, Mister Ken."

The understatement of the year. "You're different."

"Maybe. Or maybe I be just another fool like everybody else."

It's becoming increasingly difficult to keep these lines of dialogue straight. One second I'm scared out of my mind, trapped in a fond memory the next. At times, I'm angry and demanding explanations from a man I don't know, and who might very well be the product of a tired, stressed out, and hyper-imaginative mind. "Is it still raining?"

"Like cats and dogs. But even if it wasn't, you ain't got no place to go."

"I'd rather be anywhere but here at this moment."

"Where you really wanna be, Mister Ken?"

The image of my son, Charlie, pops into my mind. Fifteen years old on the outside, old as Methuselah in other ways. God, I miss him.

"Yes. The melody…"

I frown. I'm tired of his cryptic references. "I don't hear any music, old man."

"You sees memories, but that be just like seeing the music with the volume off."

I shake my head. "That makes no sense."

Morty doesn't reply but stares placidly out the window, smug as an emperor who stated his point beyond any reasonable doubt. "Melodies and memories," he whispers. "Some make you laugh. Most make you cry. And some, oh well, they just make you angrier than a caged devil."

"Yeah…" Anger marked much of my last days with Kate.

"Why'd you get so angry at Miz Kate?"

"I don't know. Guess a lot of little things just piled up on us."

Morty stares at nothing, probably lost in my thoughts. "What you mean?"

I don't reply, but I have the odd feeling I don't have to. I can almost feel Morty browsing through my memories like a shopper perusing a catalogue...

I arrived home one day to find Charlie's sad little face staring out the window. He was only six then. Inside, Kate huffed around in annoyance until I finally broke down and asked what was wrong.

"Charlie went out in his brand new school shoes. I caught him jumping in puddles, making a muddy mess. I grabbed him, spanked him, and he knows I'm so mad at him right now, I could scream!"

My heart ached for my little boy. "What is wrong with you, Kate?"

"Me?" She pointed at herself, her expression pure disbelief. "Brand new shoes!"

"But Kate, he's just a little boy. It's not like we can't afford to buy him another pair."

Kate ran a hand through her brown hair in frustration. "I am not about to spoil our son like my father did. I don't want Charlie to turn into my sisters or my best friend."

"Or you?"

Kate recoiled like she'd been hit.

"I'm sorry, I didn't mean…"

She dismissed my apology with a shake of her head. "I'm going back to work, Ken. I have to."

"Don't be ridiculous. I don't want Charlie in daycare again. That's final." I headed for the sidebar in my studio but she followed me.

"Final?"

I swallowed hard, but I wasn't about to let her take out her frustrations on my little boy. A line had to be drawn.

"Go ahead and get drunk again, Ken. Maybe you quit on your dreams, but I sure as hell didn't quit on mine."

"Oh, and our son takes a back seat to your dreams. Is that it?"

Kate's wounded expression filled me with satisfaction.

"It shows how little you know about me, Ken. My biggest dream has everything to do with you and our son."

She went into Charlie's room and sat with him for a few minutes, holding him and laying soft kisses on his head. She then stood, claimed a headache—induced by yours truly—and excused herself to our bedroom.

I left with Charlie and bought him a pair of rain boots, a slicker, and an umbrella modeled after Captain America's shield. We spent the entire afternoon jumping in the puddles at the local park.

It was one of the last times I laughed.

Hundreds of memories flash in my head. I feel like I'm watching an old film where the image spins to convey the passage of time. The roulette of my life comes to a sudden stop to the day everything changed.

The call from the board of directors telling me they sold the company spelled the end of our carefree life.

Tired of arguing and mopping puddles of whisky or vomit, and cleaning up broken glass off the floor, Kate left with Charlie and went to live with her parents. I signed off the house back to the bank and spent a week driving to Oregon.

"You damn right it was all your fault."

I nod absentmindedly.

"She ain't happy."

I scoff at this. "Her father gave her a job and a new house in Essex. Nice little place with a gorgeous view of the Connecticut river, just like she always dreamed. I think she's just fine."

Morty stares at me for a long moment before shaking his head, silently branding me for an idiot. "Is she now?"

-8-

"You did hear the melody though. Didn't you?"

The rain has tapered off. However, the thought of crossing a cemetery in the middle of the night is less appealing than staying here to try to figure out what Morty is or what he's talking about.

He glances out the window at the forlorn tombstones that rise out of the grounds like monolithic weeds. "What you afraid of? We in good company here. 'Cept for that Claire Rizzo. She a mean old so and so."

I laugh. "Morty, what are you doing to me? How do you get into my thoughts?"

"I ain't done nothing. What you think be written all over your mug. I just be a good reader."

"I don't buy it."

"I ain't selling you nothing. I just be telling the truth."

"Listen. Thanks for the tea and all, but I should get going."

"I done told you, you gots nowhere to go."

"All the same," I get up. "I shouldn't keep you from resting."

"I gots 'til kingdom come to rest, boy. I don't hear the melody no more."

"What's this melody business?"

Amber light flashes in his eyes. "It's the requiem."

"The requiem?"

"If you afraid of dying and can't listen to the melody then you might as well join Mister Rand. I'll dig you up a spot myself. Live not, feel not. Ain't that right?"

A cold chill crawls down my spine. "What are you talking about?"

"You ain't been living no more, Mister Ken."

Something is wrong. It's suddenly darker. It's so dark I can't even see the glow of Morty's eyes. "Morty? Morty! Where are you?" The only reply is silence.

When I reach out, my hand sinks into damp, soft earth. Something wet glides across my fingers and I scream as I shake the disgusting worm off my hand. "Morty!"

After only two steps, I smell the damp soil before I walk into it. "Morty! Where are you? Mor—"

A shovelful of dirt falls from above. My jaw clenches and my teeth gnash the gritty particles I'm unable to spit.

More dirt falls on my back and my shoulders. I desperately try to get away but I can't. I'm surrounded by dirt walls.

"Yous gots to lie down. It's quicker that way."

Morty's voice carries a malevolent tone. It's still dark as a crypt all around me and dirt continues to rain on me, forcing me to keep my head down. When I try to move I can't. I'm standing knee deep in hardening mud where worms wriggle like boneless fingers eager to touch me.

I claw at the dirt enclosing me only to have chunks of damp earth add to the growing mound under me. "No!"

The dirt rain stops.

"Ah, folks ain't never more alive than the moment they realize they be reading their last page. You feel alive, Mister Ken?"

"Morty, don't do this!"

A puzzled silence. "Why?"

"I don't want to die!"

"Yous don't got to. You's already dead. I just be covering you up for good measure."

This has got to be a bad dream. The most vivid nightmare ever, but all I have to do is wake up. Except...I shouldn't feel the pain of my torn nails from digging so hard. I shouldn't taste the disgusting dirt. I shouldn't smell the fetid worms wiggling all around me.

"This ain't no damn dream," Morty voices my biggest fear in a voice alien to me and as hollow as an empty grave, devoid of emotion.

"NO!"

He sends another torrent of dirt in response.

"Please! I beg you. Don't do this! Morty! Stop! Please!"

The dirt reaches my chest by the time he stops burying me. My speech grows incoherent, deteriorated by racking sobs. I can no longer move my arms or my legs.

"What you cryin' for? You think Miz Kate ain't give a rat's ass where you be now cuz she gots herself a new house? And baby boy be too tired of wondering why his daddy walked off drunk like a damn coward? You ain't gots to wonder what folks be saying if you write. Ain't no one gonna say you is no good. You ain't gonna have to wonder what Miz Kate gonna say if you says you was wrong. You ain't gonna suffer no more. Ain't it what you want? Ain't no point in living cuz it leads nowheres. Still believe that?"

"NO!"

"Ah, don't be lying to me, boy. You ain't wanna live no more. I help you get your wish."

"NO! NO! NO!"

Morty shoves more dirt and doesn't stop until it reaches my chin despite the painful stretching of my neck.

"You ain't be hearing the melody no more, Mister Ken," Morty roars the accusation. "Life's a song for everybody. Some gets sad.

Some gets happy. Some gets fucking annoying and some just be different, but they all gots an end. Life's the melody so yous better dance while you hears it, but you gone done forgot all that.

Dirt falls over my face. I try shaking my head but it's now encased in dirt. I can only open one eye to stare at the silhouetted demon about to finish me.

The moonlight outlines the contours of powerful shoulders instead of the stooped back of an old man. I can see his eyes now. They glow an angry amber that flash over a wide grin of wicked teeth that take up the entire lower half of his face and appear to glow in the dark.

Past his strangely deformed head, the starry sky is devoid of storm clouds.

I refuse to let the demon become my last image and focus on the stars above instead.

"The last things they all see is the stars. Always too late they see the light. Always too late," Morty laments as he stabs at the ground next to him with the shovel.

"Kate, I'm sorry. I still love you," I utter quickly like a prayer. "Charlie, wherever I go from here, I'm with you…always…" My voice chokes and tears disappear into the soft dirt. I want to see my boy's little grin just once more.

I want to hear the melody of his laughter.

When the last pile of dirt slides off Morty's shovel, I force my eyes to remain open despite the dirt burning them. Above me, the distant stars become the light behind the film reel of the best parts of my life.

The melody of my life.

-9-

"'Scuse me, Sir. Ain't you got a home to go to? I ain't mean no disrespect, but these folks all got to rest forever, and you being here ain't helping 'em none."

"Huh?"

"You gonna catch yourself your death in the downpour. Gots to get home."

The old man is as bent as a rusty nail in a board torn out of a wall. He fixes me with a watery, jaundiced gaze that conveys apology. "Morty?"

"Sir?"

"Is that your name?"

The black visage is as wrinkled as an old dollar bill. "That's what this here says. Ain't it?" He points a yellowed fingernail to an embroidered name tag on his khaki shirt.

"You tried to bury me." My voice quivers.

"Sir?" He looks utterly perplexed.

"What day is it?"

Morty draws back to examine me from head to toe. Confusion is etched on his face.

I glance at my watch, 3:32P.M. "What the hell…?"

"You late for something, Sir?"

The disorientation is almost too much to bear.

Above, the leaden mantle parts to allow rays of sunlight to reach the grounds. The sight of light overwhelms me to the point that I stifle a cry.

The gravedigger is clearly uneasy. "You look like you seen a damn ghost or something."

I'm shaking. Whatever happened, happened only in my head. I have to bite my fist not to sob from utter relief, but I nod at the small man. "I'm…okay…"

My hands don't smell like dirt. My fingernails aren't torn, and unlike Steve, I'm above ground. Alive. "I'm okay!"

"Well, thank the Lawd, Hallelujah, but you can't be here no more. You gots to get on home now."

"I am. I'm going home." The sun falls on the stone path that leads to the gates, a clear sign if I have ever seen one.

Morty's eyes go wide when I take his hand in both of mine. Unable to express the current of joy electrifying every cell in my body, I crush the old man to my chest and kiss his forehead. "Thank you. Thank you!"

I run, inwardly apologizing to Steve, whose song is over but I imagine wherever he is, he may actually be happy I can hear the melody again.

"God bless you, young man."

I plant my feet on the turf as my blood freezes. I've ran at least two hundred feet from him. And yet, Morty's voice was as clear as though he whispered the blessing in my ear.

He is nowhere to be found when I scan the grounds. "You too, Morty." I call over my shoulder.

-10-

Hesitation never enters my mind as I rush for the red door and knock. A curtain moves aside to reveal Kate's startled face. Even with the shock that turns her features rigid, I've seldom seen such loveliness.

When the door opens, she doesn't utter a word although I can almost hear her thoughts.

"Kate, I'm sorry."

"Why are you here, Ken?"

"Where's Charlie?"

"Kenneth," she pleads. "I don't want to do this…"

"Kate. Please."

She exhales long and slow, "He's next door, playing with his friend. Did something happen? Why are you here? Are you drunk?"

She tucks her hair behind her ear, the gesture as familiar to me as breathing, making my heart swell. "Nothing happened. Okay no. A lot's happened. I mean. I don't know what I mean, but no. I'm not drunk."

"Ken, you're scaring me."

"I'm sorry. I don't know what to say right now. I just…It's so good to see you."

Kate stays silent, her expression unreadable. "You shouldn't be here. Ken, I…"

"Please, just hear me out," I say quickly.

I won't assume she's been waiting for me to come to my senses for the last nine months. As attractive as she is, there's no way in hell someone more deserving than me hasn't discovered what a treasure she is. "Please don't listen to your instinct telling you to harden your heart. If I lost it, I will accept that, but you and I brought a little boy into this world, and all I ask of you is to grant me the chance to earn his forgiveness if not yours."

Kate's eyes turn liquid as she shakes her head and her hands squeeze the fabric of her shirt.

"Kate, Steve passed away."

She nods. "Yeah. I was at the wake. I know you must be shaken from his death, but—"

"You were at the wake?"

"Of course I was there. I was with Marney. We stayed out of sight for the obvious reasons though. She didn't think she'd be welcome at the burial."

"Kate, you're right to assume I have suddenly acquired some new perspective, and I have no way of convincing you it's much more than that."

She crosses her arms, eyebrow raised. "There's nothing you can say, Ken."

"I think you're wrong."

Her eyes find mine for only a fraction of a second before she looks away. "I'm done, Ken. We're done."

I manage to stifle the urge to sob and something inside me, some unmovable steel band around my heart, grows brittle and turns to dust. For the first time, I find my voice and don't retreat into the confines of a bottle. "Kate,

I can't stand the silence anymore. I can't live without the melody you and our son really are to my life."

Her lower lip trembles and tears spill over her lashes. She makes a desperate attempt to cover her eyes like a shamed child.

I want to envelop her in my arms. I want to hold her face close and lose myself in the depths of her soul. I want to hear her heart match the beat of my own.

The silence is deafening until it's suddenly interrupted by music. Kate frowns and turns her attention to the stereo in the living room. Shania Twain's *From This Moment,* our wedding song...

For a second, I expect her to step over to the offending machine and knock it off the table in a rage. Instead, she steps aside and silently asks me in.

"This doesn't make any sense," Kate says. "Charlie spilled a whole glass of iced tea on the stereo last weekend. It hasn't worked since."

We stare at each other, both of us trapped by the notion that an unseen force is at work. I can almost hear the easy laughter of an old man and a litany of cursing spoken with an old Mississippi lilt.

As Bryan White's voice joins Shania's, I close the distance and take Kate's hand. "I've missed you more than I ever wanted to admit even to myself."

Kate sighs. "I don't want to hurt anymore, Ken."

"I don't either, Kate."

"What exactly do you want?"

No answer will carry more importance in my life than this one. "I'd like the chance to be someone you and Charlie are proud of, but I can't do that without you in my life. I don't expect you to believe me, but I know now, more than at any other point in my life, what you mean to me."

Kate lifts her face, tears streaming down the delicate planes of her cheeks.

"Kate…"

"I missed you too."

I hold her gaze and tentatively reach for her face with the back of my hand. A relieved sigh escapes me before I can speak again. "May I have this dance?"

-11-

"Hello. Glass residence." Charlie beats me to the phone.

"Who is it?"

He shushes me with a finger to his lips. "No way!"

"Who is it?"

Again, the finger to the lips. "Are you serious?"

"Charlie?"

He turns away. "I guess so, Mr. Roberts. He's right here." He finally hands me the phone. "It's your agent, Dad."

My heart skips a beat when he refers to me as "Dad". It has taken several months for my son to allow me back into his good graces. An entire week went by before he stopped looking at me like a nefarious visitor. It took another week for him to address me. "Could you pass the salt?" were the first words he said to me.

Kate worked feverishly to get Charlie to forgive me until one day we somehow found ourselves outside tossing a football.

I was doing what I could to evoke some response from him. He was polite but distant as he responded to my questions about the Patriots.

"Do you think Brady has one more Super Bowl run in him?"

Charlie stared at the football for a long moment after catching it.

I saw judgment in his eyes when he finally looked at me. I also saw hope and some sort of warning.

"Charlie, I won't leave you again."

He nodded and a tear rolled down his face.

I approached him slowly. It cut me to ribbons to be this boy's father and feeling unable to simply take him in my arms and kiss the top of his head.

"Dad?"

The lump of emotion lodged in my throat stole my voice for a moment. "Talk to me, please."

"It really sucked without you."

I nodded, unsure how to proceed but Charlie saved me by closing the distance, dropping the football, and tearfully embracing me. I swear I could see Morty's knowing grin…

"Mom! Mom!" My son's voice brings me back to the present.

I follow Charlie's dash out of the room, suddenly dreading to take the call. "Mr. Roberts?"

"Kenny, have I got news for you, my boy..."

By the time Charlie returns, dragging Kate by the hand, I've dropped the phone and slid to the floor, both my hands covering my mouth in pure disbelief.

"Lee Roberts?" Kate asks.

I nod.

"Mom, they're going to make it a movie!"

Kate squeals and collapses on top of me, dragging Charlie with her.

My novel sold, and Lee Roberts somehow got someone mad enough to make a movie out of it.

"Daddy, what's the title going to be?"

"The same as the book hopefully."

"Rek…wait, what is it again?"

"Requiem," Kate says.

"That's it. What's that?"

Kate turns to me. "Want to take this one?"

Requiem is defined as a church service for funerals where people sing their sorrow, but I'm not about to apply that definition at this moment. I think it's fair to assume a requiem can be something unique to each person. In my case, it's a reminder in the form of a melody that has one simple message: don't turn away from life.

"Dad?"

"Sorry. I was thinking, but I'm not even sure how to describe it."

"Oh." Charlie looks disappointed. "Does it have space ships?"

"Not exactly, kiddo."

"Monsters?"

"Nope."

"Total babes?"

"Charlie!" Kate cries.

"It's not for kids. Is it?"

I shake my head and smile at him. "Would it make you feel better if I told you that it's got a happy ending?"

"I guess so. Mom, can I tell Derek?

Kate nods. "Just don't brag."

Charlie rolls his eyes. "I know, I know."

When our son runs out of the room in search for the phone, Kate hugs me tight and turns her face up to kiss me.

"That's my job," she says.

"You're going to brag about your man?"

"No. I'm going to brag that I'm the inspiration behind the happy ending."

"You wish."

Kate gapes at me. "Aren't I?"

"Think of the novel as a song. You and Charlie are the melody."

She thinks for a few seconds. "I looked it up. It's a mass for the dead."

I nod.

"It's not fair that you haven't let me read it, you know. Did you kill me on the page? Did you?"

I laugh. "Of course not. Someone did die though."

"Who?"

"A man you used to know."

Kate is silent for a long moment. She takes my hand and brings it to her lips before pressing her cheek against it. When she glances at me and smiles, I finally understand what Morty was talking about.

This feeling of perfect simplicity, this moment of clarity, this undeniable joy of being alive flows right through my soul, and I can clearly hear the melody in every part of me.

-12 -

On the fifth anniversary of the release of my novel—and twenty-six months after the debut at the theaters—I make my way to Stratford's Seaside Memorial Grounds. My only companions are a hardback copy of *Requiem*, and an overwhelming sense of gratitude.

The wipers worked full time to give me a glimpse of the road the whole way down from Essex, but the skies finally clear by the time I pull into the cemetery's drive.

Several sedans file out of the grounds, friends and relatives of the recently departed. A woman stands alone next to a small mountain of flowers by a row of chairs under a tarp. The man in the khaki uniform walking away from the new grave is not Morty.

Memories of that strange series of events still make me shudder.

"Excuse me," I call.

The man is a husky, middle age man. His beard is neatly trimmed and stained by the smoke of the pipe he bites. "Can I help you?"

"Yes. I'd like to see Morty. He works here."

The man rubs his chin in thought. "I've never hired anyone named Morty, but you're not the only one looking for him."

"He was here about five years ago."

"What'd he look like?"

I describe him with all the flair of an author, but the man, Ron Wilcox, has never met Morty.

"Five years ago, you say?"

I nod. "Five or six."

The man thinks back for a minute. "Hmm. Follow me."

A strange buzzing starts in my head. I don't know why I even felt the need to come in the first place.

The ground is soft beneath me, too soft. To make matters worse, I can smell the moist ground and my mind flashes to pinkish forms writhing over my body.

I stop to shut my eyes and try to focus on a moment with my wife and son which fills me with a sense of calm.

"You alright?"

"Yes. Sorry. I'm not wearing the right shoes for this."

The man nods. "Spring showers turn everything to mush."

Mr. Wilcox leads me through a row of old stones leaning over the graves of their namesakes, sleepy sentinels standing guard through the years. Directly ahead of us, an old dilapidated, familiar block building missing a roof squats forlornly.

"I see you decided to demolish that old building."

Wilcox stops walking to glance at the building. "That's just what's left of the old crematorium. That building was condemned way before you and I were born."

The buzzing in my head feels like agitated wasps about to attack an intruder.

"Anyways, you asked about a Morty. I'm afraid this is the best I can do. It's the damnest thing though."

"What?"

"You are not the first person trying to find him."

"I'm not?"

"Years ago a Vietnam vet came by asking about him."

My pulse quickens.

"There was an old priest too, now that I think about it. Now you."

Wilcox steps to his right, pats the cracked top of a soot-stained tombstone, and hastily yanks the tall weeds to uncover the inscription.

I'm not exactly surprised, but I fall to my knees before the marker like a penitent man wrapped in a sense of equal parts of absolute fear and absolute wonder.

HERE LIES
MORTIMER PORTER
1819-1912

-13-

Under the relative protection of a canvas canopy, Karen Delano watches the man place a book on the headstone before walking away.

The young journalist fights her curiosity and stands rooted to the spot, watching the man wipe off tears with his sleeve before walking away. She thinks she recognizes the man and thinks about talking to him but stops herself.

She came to say goodbye to her favorite college professor and it would be disrespectful to leave, especially after having been already late.

Looking at all the tombstones, she wonders what's the point of living. It was one thing to dismiss the concept of dying at twenty, but at thirty-five, the looming destiny for everyone scares her.

Before she begins to fidget, she digs a cigarette out of her purse and is about to light it when a voice startles her.

"'Scuse me, Miz. Ain't you gots no home to go to? Morty don't mean no disrespect, but these folks all gots to rest forever, and you being here ain't helpin' 'em none."

Javier A. Robayo

ABOUT THE AUTHOR

Javier A. Robayo immigrated to the United States in 1988, and began writing as a way of learning English. He lives in Connecticut with his wife and two daughters, where he's busily typing the hours away to bring you his next novel.

For more information on his work, please visit:

www.javierrobayoauthor.com
or
Javier A. Robayo, Novelist
on Facebook

Turn the page for more…

The Gaze

As a sophomore in college Samantha Reddick meets Tony Amaya, a brokenhearted young man, whose written words she keeps as a memento of a weekend long affair. The words, written on the back of a paper placemat, become her only solid ground during a tumultuous decade that nearly destroys her, leaving her searching for answers at the bottom of the bottle.

Haunted by guilt and the constant menace from a man she once loved, Samantha searches for Tony and inserts herself into his life through an online friend request to his wife, Gwen. Mutual curiosity opens the door to an unexpected friendship that becomes the catalyst of an inner battle between the better woman Samantha longs to be, and the Samantha who despises her own gaze.

Praise for *The Gaze*

"…the characters frustrated me, which is also a testament to Robayo's genius. I wanted to pluck almost all of them off the page at different times and give them a good shake for their poor choices, choices that I've unfortunately witnessed people I know make. Robayo's characters are flawed, broken, and deceive themselves in their true motives, just as real flesh-and-blood people do. But despite their deficiencies, they also possess enduring and noble qualities. These traits are portrayed especially well in Samantha's relationship with her childhood friend, Lewis. Everyone should have a friend like Lewis."

-Elise Stokes author of *Cassidy Jones Adventures* hit series.

"The style is fluid and fresh which made me feel I was watching a movie. This is a first rate modern romance with a cutting edge and I enjoyed it very much."

-Emma Calin British author of *Knockout.*

"…this was more of a five-star experience than it was a book!"

-Jan Romes author of *The Gift of Gray*

"Rarely does a book grab me from the very beginning and pull me seamlessly through the whole story to leave me satisfied at the end, but wanting more."

-John W. Huffman award winning author of *Above All*

"Having read hundreds, perhaps thousands, of books in my life, never has there been one this impactful, this vastly memorable, this addictive...for me."

-Jo Vonbargen author of *This Far Time*

Turn the page for an excerpt…

Night gave way to daylight as he talked about Gwen and the odd circumstances that had found them together. I listened raptly to each word as he painted the images so clearly, I could see and feel everything.

Gwen was engaged herself when they met, while Tony had broken his engagement to a longtime girlfriend. It was obvious they were too young to know what they wanted in a life partner, perhaps rushed by a sense of obligation to their respective exes.

There was venom as Tony spoke of the nameless other. The story wasn't unfamiliar. The lass had used every method of manipulation to control his every thought. It was monstrous. In retrospect he saw the relationship was doomed from the second her parents felt it was their duty to mold their futures. They threw psychological obstacles and enough emotional duress, like some kind of sick endurance test, before granting their blessing. When the pressure drove them apart, the girl found herself in the arms of another. The pain had nearly broken Tony.

He admitted at being no saint himself once he'd discovered her infidelity and soon set off in a series of deeds aimed at inflicting as much pain as possible. The aftermath of their break up was ugly in the way nuclear fallout is ugly. He had only been able to piece himself together after finally walking away from her, though she swore to never release him.

Meanwhile, Gwen had been engaged to someone else for all the wrong reasons. Tony knew her only from the bank where she worked as a teller but the attraction had been instantaneous.

Gwen had unexpectedly appeared at a college party and before any of the many hungry blokes surrounded her in an attempt to score, Tony had stepped in and asked her to dance. In the midst of a ballad, she had confessed her feelings for him and before he knew what to say, she'd kissed him. He hadn't been the same since.

"I figured I was some sort of last hurrah, you know? Like, I was her bachelorette party of sorts. I mean, she was getting married." He shook his head. "I even had a feeling it was some brutish, linebacker, lawyer type. It had to be someone successful because she was just so beautifully elegant and delicate, and I couldn't imagine anyone less than that being with her. I sure as hell couldn't imagine her with someone like me."

"It sounds to me like you were both attached to the wrong persons."

"I know I was. But imagine my shock when the next night Gwen shows up with no ring on her finger. She simply came right up to me, pulled me out to dance and threw her arms around me. We kissed like we'd been together for years instead of one night."

"You were waiting for each other," I offered.

He went on to speak of that night, the two of them just talking, kissing sporadically. He was perfectly content just being in the same room with her. He could barely believe his luck as this blue eyed beauty pulled him out of despair and loneliness. I smiled at the tilt in his voice as he described her. It was surreal to hear a guy talk about the things I was experiencing with him right at that moment, only he was talking about another girl.

You are a masochist, Sam…

Soon I had this picture in my head of this amazing girl that so clearly captured his heart. I knew then I would simply let go. It saddened me to think that way but I had imposed upon a very delicate situation here, and pride dictated for me not to be a rebound girl. I was suddenly eager to board that plane to London.

Sensing my inner battle, he asked about me and I did less than fill the blanks. There was no point really.

Once again he promised he wasn't trying to use me and I loved him for it. Before my heart shattered anymore, I turned my face up to kiss him. I let my lips linger upon his as his arms grew tighter around me.

He whispered that I was beautiful and it didn't feel as a product of the moment. I had always thought I was pretty in a subtle way, but the way he looked at me as he called me beautiful, made me feel like I glittered.

As the kiss grew more heated, more expressive of renewed need, I sensed a revelation I hoped wouldn't materialize. It took root within me in a hidden corner of my soul.

I could love him. I could.

I could lose myself in his strong, warm embrace and find the harbor I sought for so long. I wanted that safety from the perilous sail my life had been, in this rudderless vessel I'd become. His touch had me falling headlong into that haven.

I could love him, perhaps I already did. I felt it each time our eyes met. I could love him even though I knew I wasn't his one. I could love him even though he wasn't mine to claim.

Nothing was going to stop me from having him for that one moment. Although I dreaded the coming loneliness and the gnawing self-reproach, I took him once again and gave myself to him freely, and to hell with the consequences…

Copyright © 2013 Javier A. Robayo

The Next Chapter

In this sequel to The Gaze, the unique brand of love that's bonded Lewis Bettford and Samantha Reddick throughout their lives faces its most challenging test as a life-altering event looms in the horizon. Lewis is assailed by a sense of an impending, drastic change that's aggravated when his ex-partner Terence rips the fabric of his identity with one simple truth, precipitating a quest for his true self that will forever alter the next chapter of his life.

Praise for The Next Chapter

"If you read The Gaze, you will open The Next Chapter already fond of this cast member. You will finish reading The Next Chapter still fond and applauding. Love is all, and Javier Robayo understands its strength."
    -Kaye Vincent author of *The Treeman*

"Javier Robayo has an amazing ability to pull you into the story and not let you go until the very last page. The characters are the kind of people I would love to just sit down and have a drink with. You just can't help but like them."
    -Lanie Malone author of *Awakening the Nightmare*

"When you've cried by the second chapter you know you're in for a great story!!"
    -Kelly Washburn, CT

"All I can say is that the characters are alive! They are distinctive, vibrant, and SO full of life. No way can a person read this book and not run the gamut of emotions as the characters' portraits are crafted, relationships developed, and their lives intertwined in an authentic way, so (if you're a crier) get a box of tissue and set it close to you as you read."

-Vicki Evans, CA

"The originality surpassed anything I've read before, and weaved a brilliant storyline."

-Kristi Ayers author of *One Petal Flower*

Turn the page for an excerpt...

When Samantha calls me on Sunday morning to spend the day in Kensington with everyone, I can't get there fast enough.

The weather cooperates by withholding the promised rain in the forecast and the day is balmy overall. Brooke and Emily model every outfit I bought them; it takes quite a while. I don't try to offer another suitcase for Gwen. I simply call my shipper and arrange to send their new clothes to their home in Pennsylvania.

We spend several hours in Nathan's library, which has an untouched section of children's volumes, some of them dating back to when Samantha and I were kids.

The Reddicks visited Nathan Jeffries nearly every weekend. To keep their only daughter out of their hair, they sometimes took me along. Samantha and I always started in the library. When our mischievous natures forced Margaret to chase us out to the grounds, broom in hand, Samantha and I shared wild adventures in the woods. We swam in the fountain when the days were hot, rode a Friesian horse Nathan had for a time, and more often than not, we took a canoe out to the middle of the pond to exchange wondrous secrets.

Brooke and Emily sit and listen as I read excerpts from Frances Hodgson Burnett's *A Little Princess*. They seem to enjoy my over the top, poetic rendition of each passage.

When Emily starts to doze off, I take her to the overstuffed couch and end up napping as well when her little form curls into me, her tiny fist refusing to let go of my shirt.

When I wake, I see Brooke reading Astrid Lindgren's *Pippi Longstocking* by lamplight.

"Brooke, what time is it, luv?"

Brooke peers up at me from behind designer reading glasses that make her look decidedly older.

"It's after dinner, but Mom said not to wake you, guys."

"I missed dinner?"

"Yeah," she cocks her head to the side as though debating something. "And I'm not supposed to tell you, but Sam took a few pictures of you to post them on Facebook."

"She did, did she?"

Brooke nods, chuckling. "Mom also said that if Emily won't go to bed tonight, she's yours to keep."

I can't think of a harsher punishment, but I suppose it's just. Emily becomes pretty wild right before bed, and I'm still smarting from her sugar high and subsequent crash from the night after our trip to the zoo.

"What do you think of Pippi?"

Brooke keeps her eyes on the page long enough to finish what she's reading before answering.

"Oh, she's great! But it's kind of funny."

"What's funny, luv?"

"Well, I'm on page one-oh-three and I have yet to know what town she lives in, they never mention it."

"Really?"

"I'm quite sure."

I'm quite sure spoken in a nearly flawless, clipped British accent.

"You must be a fast reader."

She shrugs. "Daddy and I have reading races. We used to read-race with Dr. Seuss books, but I don't think he realized I know most of them by heart." She grins confidently. "I always win."

"That makes me think of Sam."

"Oh, I want to be just like her when I grow up."

I actually feel my heart stutter at that. "Young lady, I've a feeling you'll be far better."

"You think so?"

I nod. "I know so."

"Lewis, can I tell you something?"

"But of course."

Two pink circles appear high on her delicate cheeks. "You're going to be an awesome daddy one day."

I hold the smile in place, but I feel something breaking inside and I most definitely cannot trust my voice to emit a steady stream of words.

"I mean it, and I'm not talking about all the stuff you got me and Em. It's just the way you are. I'm going to hate going back home and I'm going to miss you like crazy."

Whoever believed grown men don't cry was never subjected to a sentiment delivered with such sincerity and heartfelt emotion, from a young lady such as Brooke Amaya.

Swallowing the lump threatening to bring me to tears, I take a deep, shaky breath and somehow manage to compose myself. I've never been this much of a sentimental wreck. "I'll miss you too, but we'll see each other more than you think."

Her hazel eyes deepen with emotion. "You promise?"

I cross my heart. "I promise."

She smiles contentedly and turns her eyes back to the page. When I get to the door, I hear Brooke padding behind me.

"Lewis?"

I turn back. "Yes, little luv?"

"Thank you for the fun day, and all my new clothes." She leans in, wrapping her arms around me.

"You're very welcome."

"I love you. You know that?"

Tears sting my eyes and I know then I will forever be a part of her life. "I love you too, little luv."

She squeezes once more before going back to her book.

"Don't worry about Em," she says over her shoulder. "She'll probably wake in a bad mood. I'll come get Mom when she does."

"You're a good sister."

She gives me an exaggerated shrug. "I try."

I walk down the hall to the kitchen where the laughter of three women echoes off the high ceiling. I can hear Alicia and Gwen debating the endless arguments of the quirks of men in every marriage. They are giving Samantha a litany of dire warnings of how her life will change, and what to expect after exchanging the "I do's".

Normally I'd saunter in and seamlessly join into the conversation, but I feel strange inside.

I leave a text message in Samantha's mobile, telling her I have a work emergency, and quietly leave to go back to my flat. I kept hearing Terence's voice the entire time I drove.

When I get home, all I can do is get out of my clothes, and stand under the hot spray of the shower just so I can kid myself by pretending that I'm not crying, even as I fall to my knees racked by my sobs.

I'm not prone to such displays of emotion, but something in little Brooke's words have torn something loose in me. It feels as though I'm seeing light through the crack of an obscured window, and learn what a sunrise is for the first time.

John & Ezekiel

When John MacGregor is left with nothing to believe, would his sorrow keep him from seeing a message of hope?

Praise for John & Ezekiel

"Javier A Robayo does it again...In John and Ezekiel, he manages to churn up such strong emotions, that I found it hard not to shake my e-reader in lieu of shaking some sense into the main character. The heaviness of what John carries around, escaped the pages and weighed on my heart."

-C.F. Winn award winning author of *SUKI*

"If you're feeling down, turn to this. It is simple, but a neat treat for the soul."

-Kaye Vincent author of *The Treeman*

"Well-written and compelling."

-Elise Stokes author of *Cassidy Jones Adventures* hit series.

"A recovering, practicing or failed Catholic, depending on how I label myself on any given day, I couldn't help but be touched by this short piece. Javier's voice is so strong and clear; his emotion so palpable."

-Peggy Jessup, NY

"Very well written short story that takes you to follow the protagonist's inner struggles with faith and life."

-Cinta Garcia de la Rosa author of *The Funny Stories of Little Nani*

Turn the page for an excerpt…

For more than a week, I did nothing. I moved around the nearly empty house like a ghost who never crossed into the light, forever chained to haunt what was once a home.

Everywhere I looked evoked a memory of happier times. This had once been our home. Jodi and I brought our baby girl to this house, completing the formation of its soul. Her first giggles had echoed in the bedroom that Jodi and I had so lovingly prepared for her arrival. I fell to my knees under the onslaught of regret, clutching Marie's first blankets before I boxed them.

From the window facing the backyard, I watched despondently as strangers disassembled Marie's playground set and took it away. I was so angry I had to fight the urge to burn the money they paid for it.

***

Jodi and Marie visited me through the computer. Our online chats allowed me to hide what I was really feeling or so I thought.

My parents were taking good care of them, as I knew they would. I avoided answering any questions about when I'd join them. I had a feeling I would never see them again. That particular thought didn't scare me. It actually brought a reprieve from the torture in my mind.

I didn't bother with eating or sleeping. I certainly didn't bother calling or seeing anyone.

If anybody came to check on me, I managed to pull away, making some excuse to stop the conversation from venturing too deeply into my state of mind.

I felt entitled to my depression. I felt a sense of justice when some memory ripped me apart during my feeble attempts to pack. I made a habit of fleeing for the street when the pain became unbearable.

The mailbox was filled with ads and official-looking remittances that I cast into the fireplace before I even bothered to open.

One of the envelopes held a letter that contained the adjustment for inflation on my life insurance policy. Jodi stood to receive over five hundred thousand dollars if I met an untimely demise. I thought I saw a light at the end of the tunnel, reasoning that five hundred grand would be enough for Jodi to buy a home and send Marie to college.

Jodi was a great mother, an incredible woman, and it'd be easy for her to lure another man into her life. She deserved someone who was able to take care of her and our daughter. That someone was obviously not me.

Without a second thought, I placed the letter in the same folder with the policy and left it in the safe. I wrote a letter that was simple and to the point then I grabbed the keys and ignored the seatbelt chime.

The plan was simple: drive as fast as possible…

And let go…

Javier A. Robayo

My Two Flags
I pledge allegiance…

Antonio Amaya's life revolved around his family, his friends, and one dream: to live in the United States. When the dream becomes reality, the drastic change creates daunting challenges.

Antonio endures exclusion and disdain from his new schoolmates by turning his disillusionment inward. Yearning to belong, he fills the pages of his notebook in the hopes of learning English.

But how does a thirteen-year-old overcome language barriers, racial slurs, and bullying while hiding his desire to return to his country from his parents, who have given up everything to live under two flags?

Praise for My Two Flags

"The story packs an emotional punch. Mr. Robayo has the gift that few authors possess: the ability to tell a story which somehow transforms the reader into the story."
-Bibliophile, TX

"Javier Robayo's book is a lesson in values, perseverance and faith in humanity."
-Karen Dydzuhn columnist for *The Fairfield Sun*

"Students would benefit from Antonio's perspective and would be unable to remain distant from witnessing bullying around them. I think the story is unique and untold in today's schools. I recommend My Two Flags without reservation."
Amy King school social worker, CT

"Javier Robayo's artful prose flows effortlessly onto the page, tugging at your every emotion and memory of being a teenager struggling to belong. It is a genuine piece of work and you can expect more from this talented young author!"

N.K. *Fairfield University Bookstore, CT*

Turn the page for an excerpt…

The morning started out like any other. Paola and I took the bus into the *Palacio de Gobierno*—Ecuador's White House— section of Quito, right in the heart of the Historic District. Within forty minutes, the bus dropped us off by the post office, which shares the same block as the Palace.

I left Paola in the capable hands of Mother Clarita then walked across the street to the antique doors of *Colegio Gonzaga*.

After singing the national anthem, Father Fernandez led us in prayer before marching to our classrooms. Mr. Ramirez, a good-humored man in his fifties with a genuine passion to teach, gave us five minutes to chat then we hit the Algebra book.

Right before the period ended, Father Fernandez entered the classroom. As required, we stood up at attention in respectful greeting.

Father Fernandez, was a gaunt old man whose shoulders stooped under the weight of his responsibilities as director to the one of the best schools in the city, second only to its sister school *Colegio San Gabriel*. I never saw him smile, but he looked grimmer than usual as he shuffled up to our teacher to deliver a hushed message. He then left without a word.

"Boys, collect your books and leave for home immediately. Riots have broken out in the city."

On the street, people ran in every direction as thick clouds of tear gas billowed just two blocks away from school. Several people turned away and ran towards the relative safety of the churches, but the priests had already locked the doors, denying sanctuary. I made a beeline across the street to the side gate of *La Providencia* to get my sister.

We had no time to figure out why the schools wouldn't just lock the doors and keep the kids inside. The buildings were practically medieval fortresses.

I heard sirens and bull horns in the distance. Not too far, three blocks away at most. I only had minutes before the riot swept into the area. I elbowed my way to the gate, screaming my sister's name at the frazzled nuns guarding the doors.

My sister confirmed my identity and the nun pushed her to me. I grabbed Paola's hand and ran without looking back. We had no time to mutter assurances.

Ideally, I wanted to cut around *Plaza de la Independencia* and away from the riot, but an encroaching mob made that impossible. The sight of men in rag masks, pumping their fists, and screaming obscenities chilled my blood.

The melee quickly escalated into a war with the police. The uniforms showed up in riot gear, helmets, shields, truncheons, ready to use brutal force to subdue the unruly masses. They began taking control of the streets with a volley of tear gas and rubber missiles fired from their vehicles.

"What's happening?" Paola asked fearfully.

"I don't know, but we're going to get out of this quick. Don't let go of my hand."

She nodded and allowed me to drag her.

Only a block away from where we were trying to run, the protestors overturned vehicles and burned tires to counter the effects of the tear gas clouds billowing around them.

Paola started coughing and rubbing at her eyes.

"No! Don't rub your eyes! Come on, this way."

I pulled her around the pathetic barricades the protestors set up. I knew it was just a matter of time before the debris was pushed out of the way by armored police tractors.

I had to keep us away from the trucks equipped with high pressure water jets, which police used to disperse rioters by knocking them down and pushing them onto the streets like refuse. I feared if Paola and I got hit by the water jet, we had no chance of holding on to one another.

As it was, the situation grew worse.

The rioters launched Molotov cocktails into the fray. I watched them force motorists out of their cars to syphon the gasoline out of the tanks so they could make the homemade fire bombs, usually liquor glass bottles filled with gasoline. The rioters used the alcohol to soak strips of clothes to plug the bottles, and use them as wicks.

Their attempts to set police vehicles on fire were nothing but a minor irritation for the armored trucks, though a real concern for the businesses that lined the streets.

Paola and I ran just before police officers charged the crowds beating down kids, old men, and women at will. They dragged bloodied innocents into a detention truck and carted them off to jail. I knew they would be released only after the family paid a hefty fine most could ill afford.

"I'm scared!"

My little sister's frightened voice tore me inside. "Run!"

I pulled Paola towards the Plaza, running past the Presidential Palace. The place teemed with people running in all directions as the angry chants of the protestors grew louder, which meant they were heading in our direction.

The far end of the plaza presented an escape in the shape of a large building I knew contained a shopping mall. At the very least, I figured we could avoid the riot by running through it. It would take us one block away from the melee but of course, I wasn't the only person with that idea.

A man screamed to my left and I heard the sickening sound of something hard hitting flesh. The man bled from the head and collapsed in the arms of two officers, who dragged his unconscious body away. One of them held a white truncheon spattered with blood.

The crowd immediately shifted in the direction of the mall, away from the police. I rode the human wave, squeezing Paola's arm, terrified of losing her.

Suddenly, people shifted back towards the plaza and we found ourselves walking against the current. From the other side of the street, a wall of black, acrid smoke rolled through the crowd. The stench of burning tires burned my throat, but we were too close to the mall to turn back.

Rocks, bricks, and flaming glass bottles full of gasoline rained over the jostling crowd. We were shoved and pushed around by others fleeing the building. I feared getting trampled or losing my grip on my little sister.

Paola's eyes widened with terror, but I ignored her cries, trying to hold it together by a very thin thread. Before we froze in place, I raised my backpack to narrow her view, like blinders on a horse to keep her focused in one direction, and urged her on.

"I'm scared," she cried again in a tremulous voice that cut into me.

I put an arm around her, drawing her closer to me. "We just have to go through *El Pasaje*

Amador, okay? Just a little more. Come on!" I urged, coaxing her to run a little faster for the entrance to the mall.

A water truck extinguished the small fires started by the protestors, who took the opportunity to attack the vehicle. I heard glass breaking as the truck retreated. The police retaliated swiftly and ruthlessly by firing teargas and rubber missiles, panicking the mob.

An older woman in front of us moved her heavy frame as fast as she could. She carried a plastic basket full of potatoes and other groceries. I slowed down to walk behind her when suddenly, a splash of blood spouted in the air. The woman dropped in front of us, unmoving.

I had the presence of mind to cover Paola's face and run around the unfortunate woman. I managed not to stop until finally reaching the entrance to the building.

Paola's eyes looked red, irritated by the noxious tear gas. My eyes fared no better. I couldn't draw more than a teaspoon of oxygen at a time. The stinging of the gas produced thick gobs of acidic phlegm that clogged my nose and throat. I felt like I'd breathed pool water with too much chlorine.

Loud blasts echoing in the building from the street made me dismiss the horrid discomfort. I urged Paola through the mall, where shopkeepers pulled down metal doors to protect their businesses. Not one person offered us protection.

We ran out of the mall, onto Venezuela Street and kept running towards Sucre Avenue, thankful for the clean air slowly cleansing our ravaged lungs. We didn't stop running until we got to the bus terminal at *La Marin*. Only then, we slowed down to hobble on sore feet from running in the stupid dress shoes we had to wear. The stiff rim around my heel chaffed the skin and with the adrenaline ebbing, the pain quickly became intolerable.

Paola kept crying, but I was not about to try to calm her. I wanted her to flush the tear gas out of her eyes.

We put our heads down against the dusty gusts hitting our faces from the speeding cars on *Avenida Oriental,* and trudged on the sidewalk for another two kilometers. Our neighborhood was just at the top of a long concrete stairway ahead.

Paola cried all her tears and walked beside me like an automaton, one little foot in front of the other. That blank look in her eyes would haunt me for the rest of my life each time my subconscious forced me to relive the nightmare.

I encouraged her to go on, and even tried to joke around to break her out of her shock, but she didn't respond. I had my own problems trying to forget the sight of the fallen woman.

My shoulders sagged with relief at the sight of our house. All I wanted was to see Mom so I could stop pretending to be brave. I wanted the comfort of her arms around me. I wanted to forget the terror that gripped me, namely those unforgettable images of sadistic cops dragging bloodied people away.

The door was locked, and my incessant knocking failed to bring my mother to the door. She wasn't home.

A spark of anger gave way to an inferno of hatred. We were two kids trying to get home from school, nothing more. And why didn't our schools shelter us from the riot? No sooner did they push the last student into those streets than they shut their heavy doors and washed their hands of us. Were we not their responsibility?

We had nothing to do with whatever the government did wrong in the protestors' eyes. We had nothing to do with the discontent of the barbarians that itched to lay devastation to the city, but only succeeded in calling forth the wrath of the demented police force.

Some of my older friends bragged about their adventures at the riots. They thought themselves big and brave for antagonizing the police by throwing rocks at their vehicles. I was sure none of them had seen a woman struck in the head by one of those rubber missiles before their very eyes.

And Mom was probably trying to get to us... An icy current of fear replaced my outrage and dropped me to my knees as the image of the fallen woman morphed into my mom in my mind.

There had been no way to warn her. We didn't have a telephone at home.

"Where's Mom?" Paola's voice echoed my fear.

"Maybe she went to the store, Pao. She'll be here soon."

After an hour, I couldn't take it anymore. I had to find Mom.

It took a lot of convincing for Paola to begin walking again but just as we made it halfway down the block, Paola wrenched her hand free and ran into Mom's open arms.

I stared at her through tears of relief.

When we finally sat safely at our kitchen table, I sagged tiredly, angry that Mom had even thought of going into that mess. When she questioned me about the events of that morning, I was unable to relate what I'd seen. I just wanted the images purged from my mind. We were safe, which was all that mattered.

The riot spread throughout the city that evening. Even the news called it the worst ever in the history of Quito.

Mom tried to explain to me why these conflicts happened, but I never really understood. Riots were just part of life in Ecuador. Ugly scenes of clashes between police and rioters dominated the news at any given time, but none of those images in our small black and white TV adequately portrayed the level of terror I witnessed that morning.

As night fell, the rioting mobs moved nearer and we could hear the whistling from fired tear gas canisters piercing through the chanting of hundreds of angry voices. We spent most of the night huddled in our living room—the only room with no windows—and waited impatiently for Dad to make it home.

Mom and I didn't voice it, but I knew her thoughts were similar to mine. Dad drove a tiny pickup, a truck version of the old Mini Cooper, and rioters targeted small cars to use them as fiery barricades once they siphoned all the fuel from their tanks. The crazed mob used any means necessary to hijack small vehicles, and they hurt the drivers if they refused to give up their cars.

I felt every single second of that endless night until sometime before midnight when Dad made it home. It turned out he was stopped by the rioters but thankfully, one of them, a man from our neighborhood recognized Dad. Had it not been for the man's intervention, I'm not sure what would've happened.

***

The images stay with me even when my uncle gently takes my shoulders. "Antonio, *mijo*, I promise you those things don't happen here. I had no idea…"

At that moment, Paola and Rody run into the kitchen to show us their latest colorings. I use the interruption to excuse myself up to my room, where I try to clear my mind of the hateful memories once and for all by writing them on a notebook I have no intention of ever reading.